DATE DUE

22399

LEW

Lewis, Paul Owen
Storm boy

$15.42

Mooseheart School

STORM BOY

WRITTEN AND ILLUSTRATED BY

Paul Owen Lewis

Gareth Stevens Publishing
MILWAUKEE

A chief's son
went fishing
alone,

and a terrible storm arose.

He soon found himself
washed ashore
under a strange sky
he had never seen before.
There was a village there.
The houses, the canoes,
and even the people
were very large.

"I am a chief's son,

and I am lost.

A storm has brought me to you,"

said the boy.

"We know this. You are welcome,

son of a chief from above,"

said one who appeared like

a chief himself.

And together they entered

the largest house of all.

Inside, the house was crowded
with finely dressed people
enjoying a feast.
They gave him a blanket to wear
and a fish to eat,
but the fish was not cut up
or cooked.

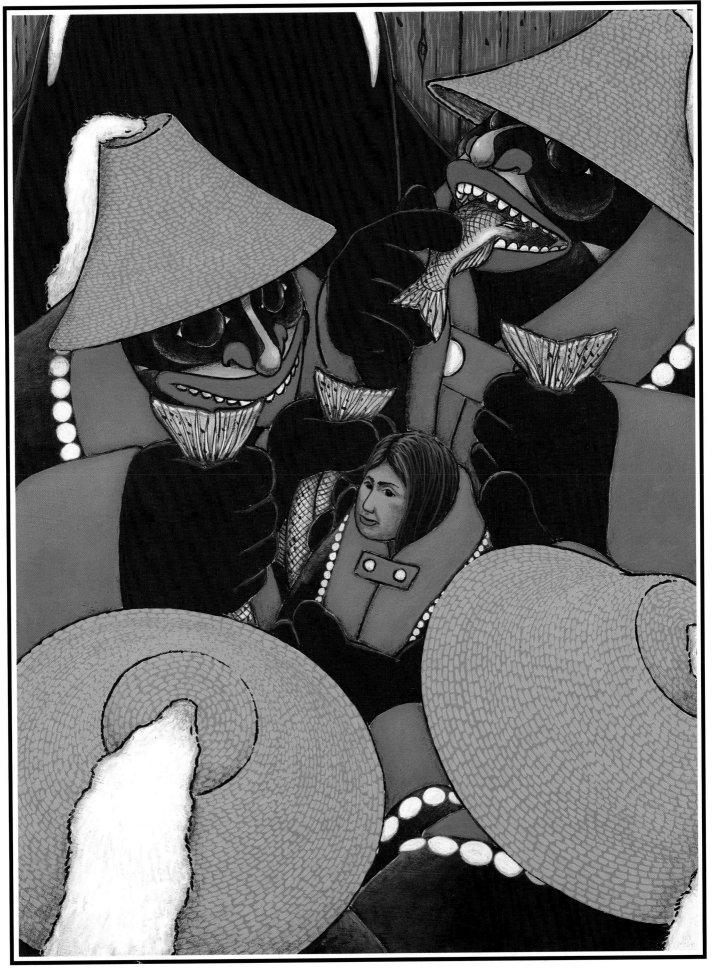

Strange, too, on the walls all around were what looked like killer whales.

After they finished eating, the chief said to the others, "Let us sing a welcome song and invite our

12

guest to join in the dance of our people."

"You are welcome! You are welcome! Son of a chief from above!" they sang.

The boy and his hosts began to dance around the fire together to the steady beat of the drums.

He matched them step for step, and the chief smiled when he saw that the boy had so quickly learned their dance.

In return, the boy offered to teach the songs and dances of his own people. The chief was delighted and now followed the boy's lead.

16

The celebration went on in this way for many long
hours, the boy and his new friends each learning
from the other.

But though the boy was enjoying himself, he began
to think more and more of home with each song he sang.

He missed his father and mother and wondered if he would ever find his way back to them again.

Suddenly, the drumming and
dancing stopped.
The chief turned to him and said,
"We are glad that the storm has
brought you to our village,
but now you are thinking
of your own."

"When you wish to return,"
he continued, "grip my staff tightly
and stand behind me.
Close your eyes and
think of your own home,
wishing to be there only."
The boy did as he was told.
He took the staff and
stepped behind the chief.
Closing his eyes,
he pictured his father and
mother, his house, and
the people of his village.

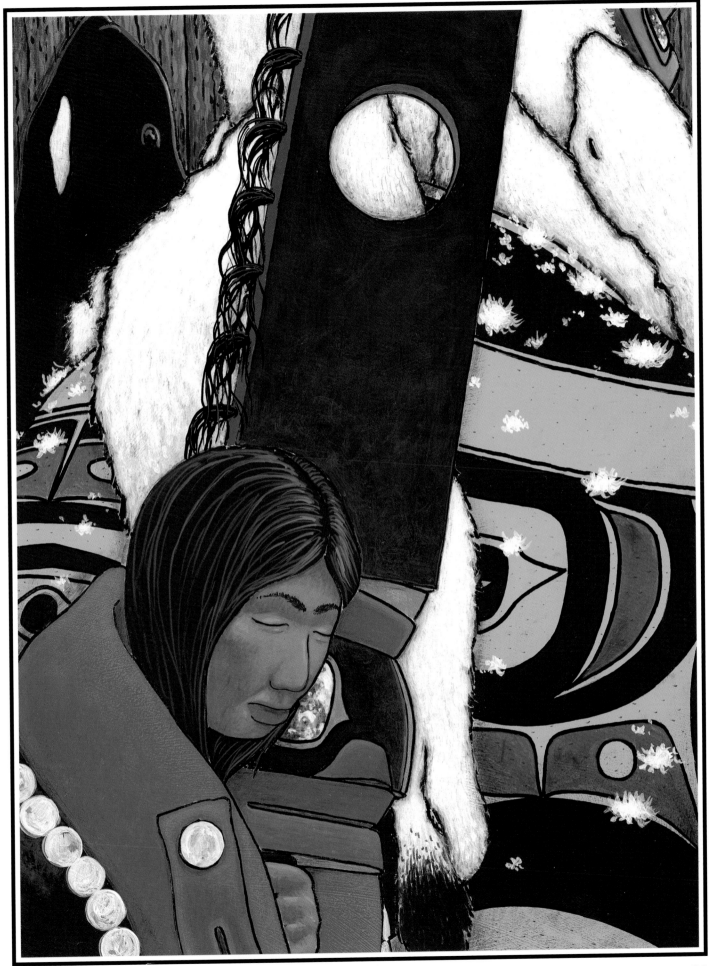

As he did, the boy felt a great surge beneath him,
as if he were being carried upward

at greater and greater speed. He kept his eyes closed
and held on tight.

The motion stopped,
and the boy opened his eyes.
There he was, lying on the beach
in front of his very own village!

"My son," cried his mother,
"where have you been? We
thought you were lost in a storm
a year ago!"

"I was lost in a storm—but it
was only yesterday!" exclaimed
the boy.

But a year's time had indeed
passed since he had disappeared
in the storm.

That night the whole village
celebrated his return and
marveled at the boy as he
danced with the staff and told
of the large and mysterious
people under the strange sky.

Author's Note

Common to all the world's mythologies is the Adventure of the Hero, whose pattern of experience renowned scholar Joseph Campbell described in three rites of passage: *separation, initiation, and return.* "A hero ventures forth from the world of common day into a region of supernatural wonder: fabulous forces are there encountered and a decisive victory is won: the hero comes back from this mysterious adventure with the power to bestow boons on his fellow man."[1] In no place is this universal theme more powerfully represented than in the rich oral traditions and bold graphic art of the Haida, Tlingit, and other Native peoples of the Northwest Coast of North America.

This cosmology held that animals possessed spirits or souls identical to human beings and were therefore referred to as *people.* There were wolf people, eagle people, and killer whale people, just as there were human people. "Animals had their own territories, villages, houses, canoes, and chiefs, and many were capable of changing into human form at will, blurring the distinction between animals and humans even more. In their own houses they used human form, and when they wished to appear in their animal form they put on cloaks and masks and spoke their animal language. The myths frequently tell of heroes being escorted by spirit beings through cosmic doorways beyond which lie villages of people who at some stage betray the fact that they are really bear people or salmon people."[2] *Storm Boy* is just such an adventure, reflecting Campbell's three rites of passage with event-motifs unique to Northwest Coast lore.

In an effort to present a degree of authenticity in the telling, a picture-book format has been deliberately chosen in which the text or verbal content is spare and the bulk of the culturally significant detail is communicated by the art. Therefore, for those readers interested in or unfamiliar with Northwest Coast culture and art, I offer the following outline and elaboration:

Northwest Coast motifs of
SEPARATION

• *Wandering too far from the village invites supernatural encounters.*
The boy is out of sight of his village and in bad weather. His identity is indicated by the style of the canoe, which is Haida; by the text, "A chief's son"; and by his clothing—his woven cedar-bark skirt is fur-lined, a sign of wealth. Heroes were most often of high caste or rank. He is a Haida prince.

• *Mysterious entrance to the Spirit World.*
In the presence of killer whales, the boy is thrown from his canoe into the sea, passes through it, and enters into another realm below.

Northwest Coast motifs of
INITIATION

• *Animals encountered in human form.*
The grand scale of the village and the displays of killer whale crest art indicate killer whale people. The frontal pole carving indicates that it is the house of a supernatural killer whale chief—more than one dorsal fin (here there are two) indicates high rank, and the holes through the fins indicate that it is of the supernatural realm. The people are dressed in ceremonial attire, hinting that a high occasion is imminent. The boy claims his high rank as a prince and is formally welcomed by the killer whale chief.

• *Exchange of gifts and culture—"potlatching."*
Inside the house the boy notices natural killer whale forms. These are the "cloaks" that the killer whale people don to appear in the natural world. After receiving gifts of food and a blanket with a killer whale crest, the boy is taught the killer whale's dance—the most valuable of gifts and one befitting his high status. One could even argue that these are signs of his adoption by the killer whales. Dancing around the rising sparks of the cedar-wood fire, the chief punctuates this event by spreading white

eagle down from the crown of sea lion whiskers atop his headdress, an extravagant gesture of welcome. The boy, in return, gives the killer whale people a gift of equal value—knowledge of his own culture through songs and dances, thus meeting the ceremonial requirement of the potlatch. (The word *potlatch* derives from the Chinook word *patshatl*, meaning "to give away.")[3]

Northwest Coast motifs of
RETURN

• *Object given to assist return.*
As the celebration winds down, the boy remembers that he is yet—in spite of this high experience—lost and cannot see how to find his way back home. The chief intuits the boy's feelings, gives him his dancing staff (shaped like a dorsal fin), and instructs the boy to hold it tightly and to stand behind him.

• *Mysterious return by "wishing continually."*
The boy takes his position behind the chief. He is further instructed to close his eyes and visualize his home, his parents, and his own village, and he is warned to think of nothing else. The boy is obedient, and a great mystery is played out. The viewer sees what the boy cannot: the killer whale chief and his people have transformed and are ferrying the boy to the upper realm.

• *Time is out of joint.*
Most fascinating is the element of time disparity between the two realms in classic Northwest Coast hero epics: for every day spent in the Spirit World, a year passes in our own. When the motion stops, the boy finds himself in front of his own village and learns from his mother that he has been missing for an entire year. His mother's fur-lined garment, many bracelets, and abalone lip-plug mark her as a woman of high rank—the wife of a chief.

• *Claiming of a crest.*
A reunion celebration occurs at which the boy recounts his mysterious adventure and displays the killer whale staff and dance. Because of his "adoption" by the killer whale people, the boy could now rightfully claim the killer whale crest as his own to display and to pass down to his descendants. In addition, the boy would very likely exhibit greatly increased skill as a fisherman, possessing the killer whale's prowess at hunting. This in turn would bring further fame, honors, and wealth. As the generations passed, his name and story would take its place among his people's greatest legends.

Though an original creation, *Storm Boy* was carefully composed entirely of Native story elements both in its narrative and art. Special thanks belong to Bill Holm and Jay Haavik for generously sharing their knowledge and encouragement; to Chris Landon, Native cultural advisor; and to the peoples and culture of the Northwest Coast that inspired it.

A Teacher's Guide for *Storm Boy* is available from Ten Speed Press. For ordering and inquiries, contact:
> Ten Speed Press
> P.O. Box 7123
> Berkeley, California 94707
> (510) 559-1600
> (510) 524-1052 (fax)

[1] Joseph Campbell, *The Hero with a Thousand Faces* (Princeton University Press, 1948) p. 30.
[2] George F. MacDonald, *Haida Monumental Art* (University of British Columbia Press, 1983) p. 6-7.
[3] Norman Bankcroft-Hunt, *People of the Totem* (University of Oklahoma Press, 1979) p. 51.

For Kyle and LeAnn

A portion of the proceeds from this book is donated to the Haida Gwaii Rediscovery program for tribal youth.

For a free color catalog describing Gareth Stevens Publishing's list of high-quality books and multimedia programs, call 1-800-542-2595 (USA) or 1-800-461-9120 (Canada). Gareth Stevens Publishing's Fax: (414) 225-0377.

Library of Congress Cataloging-in-Publication Data

Lewis, Paul Owen.
Storm boy / written and illustrated by Paul Owen Lewis.
p. cm.
Originally published: Hillsboro, Oregon: Beyond Words Pub., © 1995.
Summary: Thrown from his canoe during an ocean storm, a young Native American boy is washed ashore under a strange sky near a village inhabited by very large people who make him very welcome.
ISBN 0-8368-2229-3 (lib. bdg.)
1. Indians of North America—Northwest, Pacific—Juvenile fiction.
[1. Indians of North America—Northwest, Pacific—Fiction. 2. Killer whales—Fiction. 3. Whales—Fiction.] I. Title.
PZ7.L58765St   1998
[Fic]—dc21   98-21284

This edition first published in 1999 by
Gareth Stevens Publishing
1555 North RiverCenter Drive, Suite 201
Milwaukee, WI 53212 USA

First published in 1995 by Beyond Words Publishing, Inc., Hillsboro, Oregon.
Text and illustrations © 1995 by Paul Owen Lewis.

Printed in Mexico

1 2 3 4 5 6 7 8 9 03 02 01 00 99